Truth may seem, but cannot be:
Beauty brag, but 'tis not she;
Truth and beauty buried be.

To this urn let those repair
That are either true or fair;
For these dead birds sigh a prayer.

Bacon

CAPTAIN BOLDHEART
BY CHARLES DICKENS

ILLUSTRATED BY
BEATRICE PEARSE

" Invited them to Breakfast "

CAPTAIN BOLDHEART & THE LATIN-GRAMMAR MASTER

A HOLIDAY ROMANCE FROM THE PEN OF LIEUT-COL· ROBIN REDFORTH AGED 9·

BY CHARLES DICKENS

FOREWORD

THE story contained herein was written by Charles Dickens in 1867. It is the third of four stories entitled "Holiday Romance" and was published originally in a children's magazine in America. It purports to be written by a child aged nine. It was republished in England in "All the Year Round" in 1868. For this and four other Christmas pieces Dickens received £1,000.

"Holiday Romance" was published in book form by Messrs Chapman & Hall in 1874, with "Edwin Drood" and other stories.

For this reprint the text of the story as it appeared in "All the Year Round" has been followed.

CAPTAIN BOLDHEART AND THE LATIN-GRAMMAR MASTER

THE subject of our present narrative would appear to have devoted himself to the Pirate profession at a comparatively early age. We find him in command of a splendid schooner of one hundred guns, loaded to the muzzle, 'ere yet he had had a party in honour of his tenth birthday.

It seems that our hero, considering himself spited by a Latin-Grammar-Master, demanded the satisfaction due from one man of honour to another. Not getting it, he privately withdrew his haughty spirit from such low company, bought a second-hand pocket-pistol, folded up some sandwiches in a paper bag, made a bottle of Spanish liquorice-water, and entered on a career of valour.

It were tedious to follow Boldheart (for such was his name) through the commencing stages of his history. Suffice it that we find him bearing the rank of Captain Boldheart, reclining in full uniform on a crimson hearth-rug spread out upon the quarter-deck of his schooner the Beauty, in the China Seas. It was a lovely evening, and as his crew lay grouped about him, he favoured them with the following melody:

O landsmen are folly!
O Pirates are jolly!
O Diddleum Dolly,
Di!

(*Chorus*) Heave yo.

The soothing effect of these animated sounds float-ing over the waters, as the common sailors united their rough voices to take up the rich tones of Bold-heart, may be more easily conceived than described.

It was under these circumstances that the lookout at the masthead gave the word, "Whales!"

All was now activity.

"Where away?" cried Captain Boldheart, starting up.

"On the larboard bow, sir," replied the fellow at the masthead, touching his hat. For such was the height of discipline on board of the Beauty, that even at that height he was obliged to mind it or be shot through the head.

" His crew lay grouped around him "

'This adventure belongs to me," said Boldheart. "Boy, my harpoon. Let no man follow;" and leaping alone into his boat, the captain rowed with admirable dexterity in the direction of the monster.

All was now excitement.

"He nears him!" said an elderly seaman, following the captain through his spy-glass.

"He strikes him!" said another seaman, a mere stripling, but also with a spy-glass.

"He tows him towards us!" said another seaman, a man in the full vigour of life, but also with a spy-glass.

In fact the captain was seen approaching, with the huge bulk following. We will not dwell on the deafening cries of "Boldheart! Boldheart!" with which he was received, when, carelessly leaping on the quarter-deck, he presented his prize to his men. They afterwards made two thousand four hundred and seventeen pound ten and sixpence by it.

Ordering the sails to be braced up, the captain now stood W.N.W. The Beauty flew rather than floated over the dark blue waters. Nothing particular occurred for a fortnight, except taking, with considerable slaughter, four Spanish galleons, and a Snow from South America, all richly laden. Inaction began to tell upon the spirits of the men. Captain Boldheart called all hands aft, and said:

"My lads, I hear there are discontented ones among ye. Let any such stand forth."

After some murmuring, in which the expressions, "Aye, aye, sir!" "Union Jack!" "Avast," "Starboard," "Port," "Bowsprit," and similar indications of a mutinous undercurrent, though subdued, were audible, Bill Boozey, captain of the forctop, came out from the rest. His form was that of a giant, but he quailed under the captain's eye.

"What are your wrongs?" said the captain.

"Why, d'ye see, Captain Boldheart," replied the towering mariner, "I've sailed man and boy for many a year, but I never yet know'd the milk served out for the ship's company's teas to be so sour as 'tis aboard this craft."

At this moment the thrilling cry, "Man overboard!" announced to the astonished crew that Boozey, in stepping back, as the captain (in mere thoughtfulness)

THE RESCUE OF WIL-
LIAM BOOZEY.

laid his hand upon the faithful pocket-pistol which he wore in his belt, had lost his balance, and was struggling with the foaming tide.

All was now stupefaction.

But, with Captain Boldheart, to throw off his uniform coat regardless of the various rich orders with which it was decorated, and to plunge into the sea after the drowning giant, was the work of a moment. Maddening was the excitement when boats were lowered; intense the joy when the captain was seen holding up the drowning man with his teeth; deafening the cheering when both were restored to the main deck of the Beauty. And from the instant of his changing his wet clothes for dry ones, Captain Boldheart had no such devoted though humble friend as William Boozey.

Boldheart now pointed to the horizon, and called the attention of his crew to the taper spars of a ship lying snug in harbour under the guns of a fort.

"She shall be ours at sunrise," said he. "Serve out a double allowance of grog, and prepare for action."

All was now preparation.

When morning dawned after a sleepless night, it was seen that the stranger was crowding on all sail to come out of the harbour and offer battle. As the two ships came nearer to each other, the stranger fired a gun and hoisted Roman colours. Boldheart then perceived her to be the Latin-Grammar-Master's bark. Such indeed she was, and had been tacking about the world in unavailing pursuit, from the time of his first taking to a roving life.

Boldheart now addressed his men, promising to blow them up if he should feel convinced that their reputation required it, and giving orders that the Latin-Grammar-Master should be taken alive. He then dismissed them to their quarters, and the fight began with a broadside from The Beauty. She then veered round, and poured in another. The Scorpion (so was the bark of the Latin-Grammar-Master appropriately called) was not slow to return her fire, and a terrific cannonading ensued, in which the guns of The Beauty did tremendous execution.

The Latin-Grammar-Master was seen upon the poop, in the midst of the smoke and fire, encouraging his men. To do him justice, he was no Craven, though his white hat, his short grey trousers, and his long snuff-coloured surtout reaching to his heels—the selfsame coat in which he had spited Boldheart—contrasted most unfavourably with the brilliant uniform of the latter. At this moment Boldheart, seizing a pike and putting himself at the head of his men, gave the word to board.

A desperate conflict ensued in the hammock nettings—or somewhere in about that direction—until the Latin-Grammar-Master, having all his masts gone, his hull and rigging shot through and through, and seeing Boldheart slashing a path towards him, hauled down his flag himself, gave up his sword to Boldheart, and asked for quarter. Scarce had he been put into the captain's boat, 'ere The Scorpion went down with all on board.

On Captain Boldheart's now assembling his men, a circumstance occurred. He found it necessary with one blow of his cutlass to kill the Cook, who, having lost his brother in the late action, was making at the Latin-Grammar-Master in an infuriated state, intent on his destruction with a carving-knife.

Captain Boldheart then turned to the Latin-Grammar-Master, severely reproaching him with his perfidy, and put it to his crew what they considered that a master who spited a boy deserved?

They answered with one voice, "Death."

"It may be so," said the Captain; "but it shall never be said that Boldheart stained his hour of triumph with the blood of his enemy. Prepare the cutter."

The cutter was immediately prepared.

"Without taking your life," said the Captain, "I must yet for ever deprive you of the power of spiting other boys. I shall turn you adrift in this boat. You will find in her two oars, a compass, a bottle of rum, a small cask of water, a piece of pork, a bag of biscuit, and my Latin grammar. Go! and spite the natives, if you can find any."

Deeply conscious of this bitter sarcasm, the unhappy wretch was put into the cutter, and was soon left far behind. He made no effort to row, but was seen lying on his back with his legs up, when last made out by the ship's telescopes.

A stiff breeze now beginning to blow, Captain Boldheart gave orders to keep her S.S.W., easing her a little during the night by falling off a point or two W. by W., or even by W.S., if she complained much. He then retired for the night, having in truth much need of repose. In addition to the fatigues he had undergone, this brave officer had received sixteen wounds in the engagement, but had not mentioned it.

In the morning a white squall came on, and was succeeded by other squalls of various colours. It thundered and lightened heavily for six weeks. Hurricanes then set in for two months. Waterspouts and tornadoes followed. The oldest sailor on board—and he was a very old one—had never seen such weather. The Beauty lost all idea where she was, and the carpenter reported six feet two of water in the hold. Everybody fell senseless at the pumps every day.

Provisions now ran very low. Our hero put the crew on short allowance, and put himself on shorter allowance than any man in the ship. But his spirit kept him fat. In this extremity, the gratitude of Boozey, the captain of the foretop whom our readers may remember, was truly affecting. The loving though lowly

William repeatedly requested to be killed, and preserved for the captain's table.

We now approach a change in affairs.

One day during a gleam of sunshine and when the weather had moderated, the man at the mast-head—too weak now to touch his hat, besides its having been blown away—called out,

"Savages!"

All was now expectation.

Presently fifteen hundred canoes, each paddled by twenty savages, were seen advancing in excellent order. They were a light green colour (the Savages were), and sang, with great energy, the following strain:

> Choo a choo a choo tooth.
> Muntch, muntch. Nycey!
> Choo a choo a choo tooth.
> Muntch, muntch. Nyce!

As the shades of night were by this time closing in, these expressions were supposed to embody this simple people's views of the Evening Hymn. But it too soon appeared that the song was a translation of "For what we are going to receive," &c.

The chief, imposingly decorated with feathers of lively colours, and having the majestic appearance of a fighting Parrot, no sooner understood (he understood English perfectly) that the ship was The Beauty, Captain Boldheart, than he fell upon his face on the deck, and could not be persuaded to rise until the captain had lifted him up, & told him he wouldn't hurt him. All the rest of the savages also fell on their faces with marks of terror, and had also to be lifted up one by one. Thus the fame of the great Boldheart had gone before him, even among these children of Nature.

Turtles and oysters were now produced in astonishing numbers, and on these and yams the people made a hearty meal. After dinner the Chief told Captain Boldheart that there was better feeding up at the village, and that he would be glad to take him and his officers there. Apprehensive of treachery, Boldheart ordered his boat's crew to attend him completely armed. And well were it for other commanders if their precautions—but let us not anticipate.

"Arm-in-arm with the Chief"

"TWO SAVAGES FLOURED HIM
BEFORE PUTTING HIM TO THE
FIRE."

When the canoes arrived at the beach, the darkness of the night was illumined by the light of an immense fire. Ordering his boat's crew (with the intrepid though illiterate William at their head) to keep close and be upon their guard, Boldheart bravely went on, arm-in-arm with the Chief.

But how to depict the captain's surprise when he found a ring of Savages singing in chorus that barbarous translation of " For what we are going to receive, &c.," which has been given above, and dancing hand-in-hand round the Latin-Grammar-Master, in a hamper with his head shaved, while two savages floured him, before putting him to the fire to be cooked!

Boldheart now took counsel with his officers on the course to be adopted. In the mean time, the miserable captive never ceased begging pardon and imploring to be delivered. On the generous Boldheart's proposal, it was at length resolved that he should not be cooked, but should be allowed to remain raw, on two conditions. Namely,

1. That he should never under any circumstances presume to teach any boy any thing any more.

2. That, if taken back to England, he should pass his life in travelling to find out boys who wanted their exercises done, and should do their exercises for those boys for nothing, and never say a word about it.

Drawing his sword from its sheath, Boldheart swore him to these conditions on its shining blade. The prisoner wept bitterly, and appeared acutely to feel the errors of his past career.

The captain then ordered his boat's crew to make ready for a volley, and after firing to re-load quickly. "And expect a score or two on ye to go head over heels," murmured William Boozey; "for I'm a looking at ye." With those words the derisive though deadly William took a good aim.

"Fire!"

The ringing voice of Boldheart was lost in the report of the guns and the screeching of the savages. Volley after volley awakened the numerous echoes. Hundreds of savages were killed, hundreds wounded, and thousands ran howling into the woods. The Latin-Grammar-Master had a spare night-cap lent him, and a

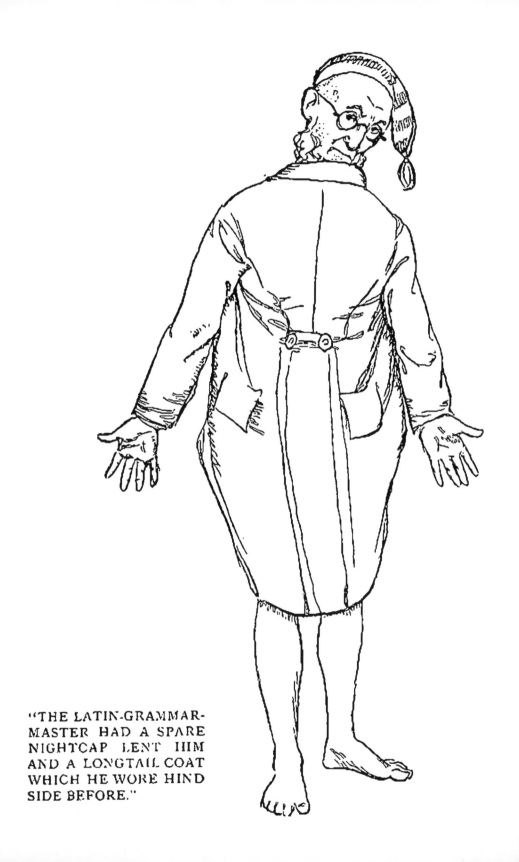

"THE LATIN-GRAMMAR-MASTER HAD A SPARE NIGHTCAP LENT HIM AND A LONGTAIL COAT WHICH HE WORE HIND SIDE BEFORE."

"ERE THE SUN WENT DOWN FULL MANY A HORNPIPE HAD BEEN DANCED . . . BY THE UNCOUTH THOUGH AGILE WILLIAM."

longtail coat which he wore hind side before. He presented a ludicrous though pitiable appearance, and serve him right.

We now find Captain Boldheart, with this rescued wretch on board, standing off for other islands. At one of these, not a cannibal island, but a pork and vegetable one, he married (only in fun on his part) the King's daughter. Here he rested some time, receiving from the natives great quantities of precious stones, gold dust, elephants' teeth, and sandal wood, and getting very rich. This, too, though he almost every day made presents of enormous value to his men.

The ship being at length as full as she could hold of all sorts of valuable things, Boldheart gave orders to weigh the anchor, and turn the Beauty's head towards England. These orders were obeyed with three cheers, and ere the sun went down full many a hornpipe had been danced on deck by the uncouth though agile William.

We next find Captain Boldheart about three leagues off Madeira, surveying through his spy-glass a stranger of suspicious appearance making sail towards him.

"Married the Chief's daughter"

On his firing a gun ahead of her to bring her to, she ran up a flag, which he instantly recognized as the flag from the mast in the back-garden at home.

Inferring from this, that his father had put to sea to seek his long-lost son, the captain sent his own boat on board the stranger, to inquire if this was so, and if so, whether his father's intentions were strictly honourable. The boat came back with a present of greens and fresh meat, and reported that the stranger was The Family of twelve hundred tons, and had not only the captain's father on board, but also his mother, with the majority of his aunts and uncles, and all his cousins. It was further reported to Boldheart that the whole of these relations had expressed themselves in a becoming manner, and were anxious to embrace him and thank him for the glorious credit he had done them. Boldheart at once invited them to breakfast next morning on board the Beauty, and gave orders for a brilliant ball that should last all day.

It was in the course of the night that the captain discovered the hopelessness of reclaiming the Latin-Grammar-Master. That thankless traitor was found out, as the two ships lay near each other, communicating with The Family by signals, and offering to give up Boldheart. He was hanged at the yard-arm the first thing in the morning, after having it impressively pointed out to him by Boldheart that this was what spiters came to.

The meeting between the captain and his parents was attended with tears. His uncles and aunts would have attended their meeting with tears too, but he wasn't going to stand that. His cousins were very much astonished by the size of his ship and the discipline of his men, and were greatly overcome by the splendour of his uniform. He kindly conducted them round the vessel, and pointed out every thing worthy of notice. He also fired his hundred guns, and found it amusing to witness their alarm.

The entertainment surpassed everything ever seen on board ship, and lasted from ten in the morning until seven the next morning. Only one disagreeable incident occurred. Captain Boldheart found himself obliged to put his cousin Tom in irons, for being disrespectful. On the boy's promising amendment, however, he was humanely released after a few hours' close confinement.

Boldheart now took his mother down into the great cabin, and asked after the young lady with whom, it was well known to the world, he was in love. His mother replied that the object of his affections was then at school at Margate, for the benefit of sea-bathing (it was the month of September), but that she feared the young lady's friends were still opposed to the union. Boldheart at once resolved, if necessary, to bombard the town.

Taking the command of his ship with this intention, and putting all but fighting men on board The Family, with orders to that vessel to keep in company, Boldheart soon anchored in Margate Roads. Here he went ashore well-armed, and attended by his boat's crew (at their head the faithful though ferocious William), and demanded to see the Mayor, who came out of his office.

"Dost know the name of yon ship, Mayor?" asked Boldheart fiercely.

"No," said the Mayor, rubbing his eyes, which he

"DOST KNOW THE NAME OF YON SHIP, MAYOR?

could scarce believe when he saw the goodly vessel riding at anchor.

"She is named the Beauty," said the captain.

"Hah!" exclaimed the Mayor, with a start. "And you, then, are Captain Boldheart?"

"The same."

A pause ensued. The Mayor trembled.

"Now, Mayor," said the captain, "choose. Help me to my Bride, or be bombarded."

The Mayor begged for two hours' grace, in which to make inquiries respecting the young lady. Boldheart accorded him but one; and during that one placed William Boozey sentry over him, with a drawn sword and instructions to accompany him wherever he went, and to run him through the body if he showed a sign of playing false.

At the end of the hour, the Mayor re-appeared more dead than alive, closely waited on by Boozey more alive than dead.

"Captain," said the Mayor, "I have ascertained that the young lady is going to bathe. Even now she waits her turn for a machine. The tide is low, though rising.

"His lovely Bride came forth"

I, in one of our town-boats, shall not be suspected. When she comes forth in her bathing-dress into the shallow water from behind the hood of the machine, my boat shall intercept her and prevent her return. Do you the rest."

"Mayor," returned Capt. Boldheart, "thou hast saved thy town."

The captain then signalled his boat to take him off, and steering her himself ordered her crew to row towards the bathing-ground, and there to rest upon their oars. All happened as had been arranged. His lovely bride came forth, the Mayor glided in behind her, she became confused and had floated out of her depth, when, with one skilful touch of the rudder and one quivering stroke from the boat's crew, her adoring Boldheart held her in his strong arms. There her shrieks of terror were changed to cries of joy.

Before the Beauty could get under weigh, the hoisting of all the flags in the town and harbour, and the ringing of all the bells, announced to the brave Boldheart that he had nothing to fear. He therefore determined to be married on the spot, and signalled for a clergyman and clerk, who came off promptly in a sailing-boat named the Skylark. Another great entertainment was then given on board the Beauty, in the midst of which the Mayor was called out by a messenger. He returned with the news that Government had sent down to know whether Captain Boldheart, in acknowledgment of the great services he had done his country by being a Pirate, would consent to be made a Lieutenant-Colonel. For himself he would have spurned the worthless boon, but his Bride wished it and he consented.

Only one thing further happened before the good ship Family was dismissed, with rich presents to all on board. It is painful to record (but such is human nature in some cousins) that Captain Boldheart's unmannerly cousin Tom was actually tied up to receive three dozen with a rope's end "for cheekyness and making games," when Captain Boldheart's lady begged for him and he was spared. The Beauty then refitted, and the Captain and his Bride departed for the Indian Ocean to enjoy themselves for evermore.

THE END.

"CAPTAIN BOLD-
HEART'S LADY BEGGED
FOR HIM AND HE WAS
SPARED."

THE ORANGE TREE SERIES OF CHILDREN'S BOOKS

FULLY ILLUSTRATED IN COLOUR. 1s. net. Foolscap 4to, boards

1 THE STORY OF RICHARD DOUBLEDICK. By Charles Dickens. With illustrations by W. B. Wollen, R.I., R.O.I.

2 THE MAGIC FISHBONE. By Charles Dickens. With illustrations by S. Beatrice Pearse.

3 THE TRIAL OF WILLIAM TINKLING. By Charles Dickens. With illustrations by S. Beatrice Pearse.

4 CAPTAIN BOLDHEART AND THE LATIN GRAMMAR MASTER. By Charles Dickens. With illustrations by S. Beatrice Pearse.

THE WONDER BOOK

By Nathaniel Hawthorne. With Coloured Illustrations by Patten Wilson.

5 THE GORGON'S HEAD   6 THE GOLDEN TOUCH

The above are ready. The following are in active preparation.

7 THE PARADISE OF CHILDREN

8 THE THREE GOLDEN APPLES

9 THE MIRACULOUS PITCHER

10 THE CHIMAERA

TANGLEWOOD TALES

By Nathaniel Hawthorne. With Coloured Illustrations by Patten Wilson.

11 THE MINOTAUR

12 THE PYGMIES

13 THE DRAGON'S TEETH

14 CIRCE'S PALACE

15 THE POMEGRANATE SEEDS

16 THE GOLDEN FLEECE

1445076R00024

Printed in Germany
by Amazon Distribution
GmbH, Leipzig